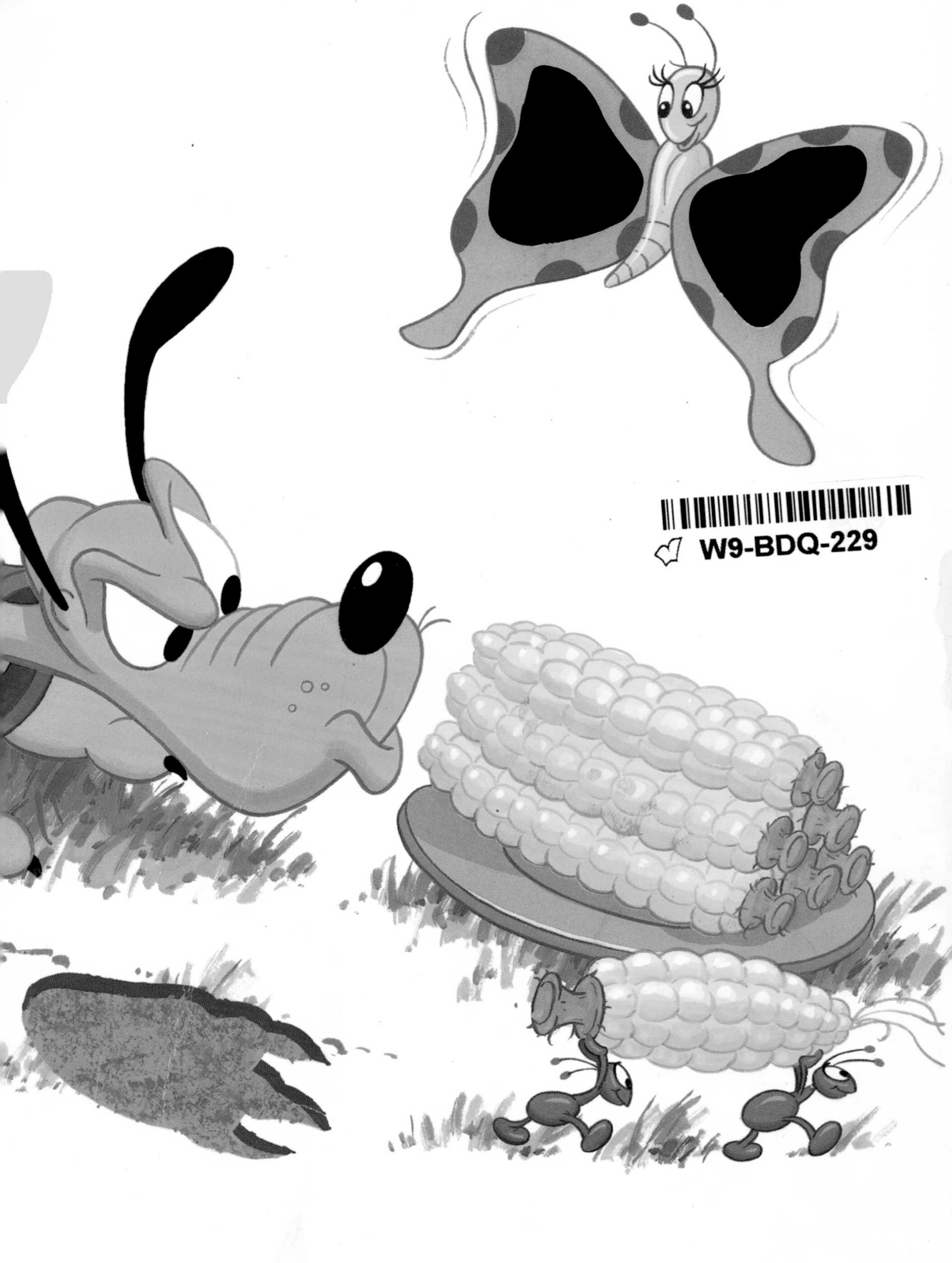

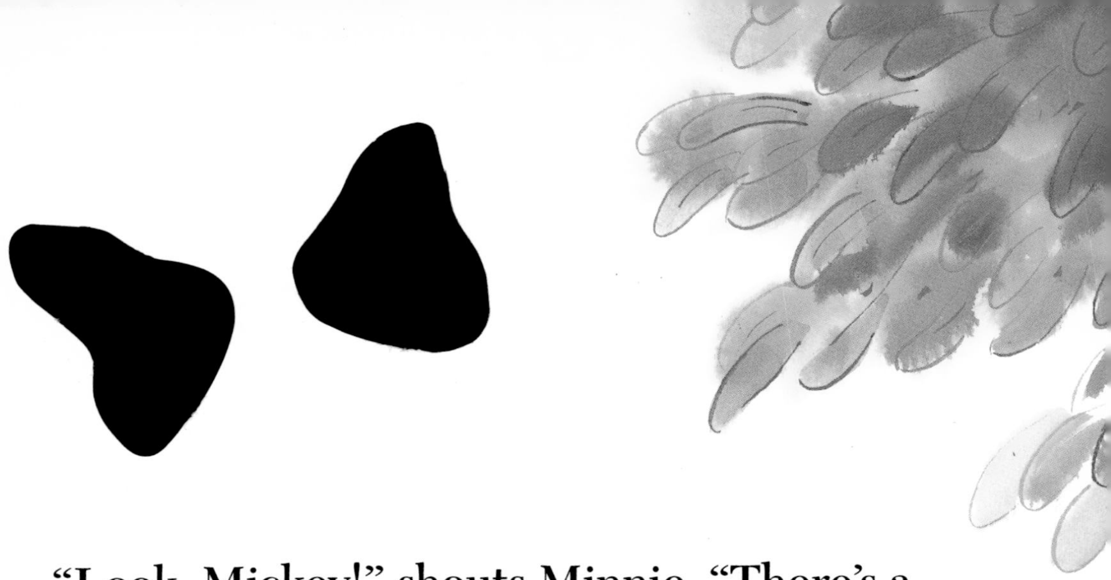

"Look, Mickey!" shouts Minnie. "There's a hole in this tree. Do you think the basket could be in here?"

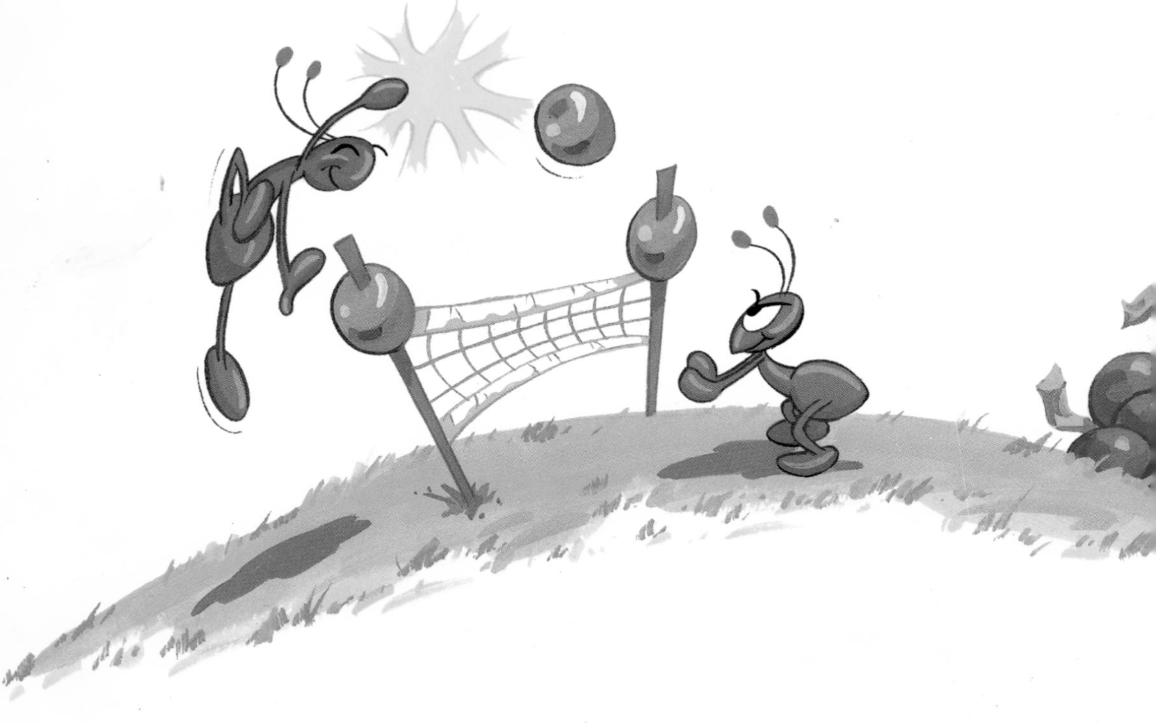

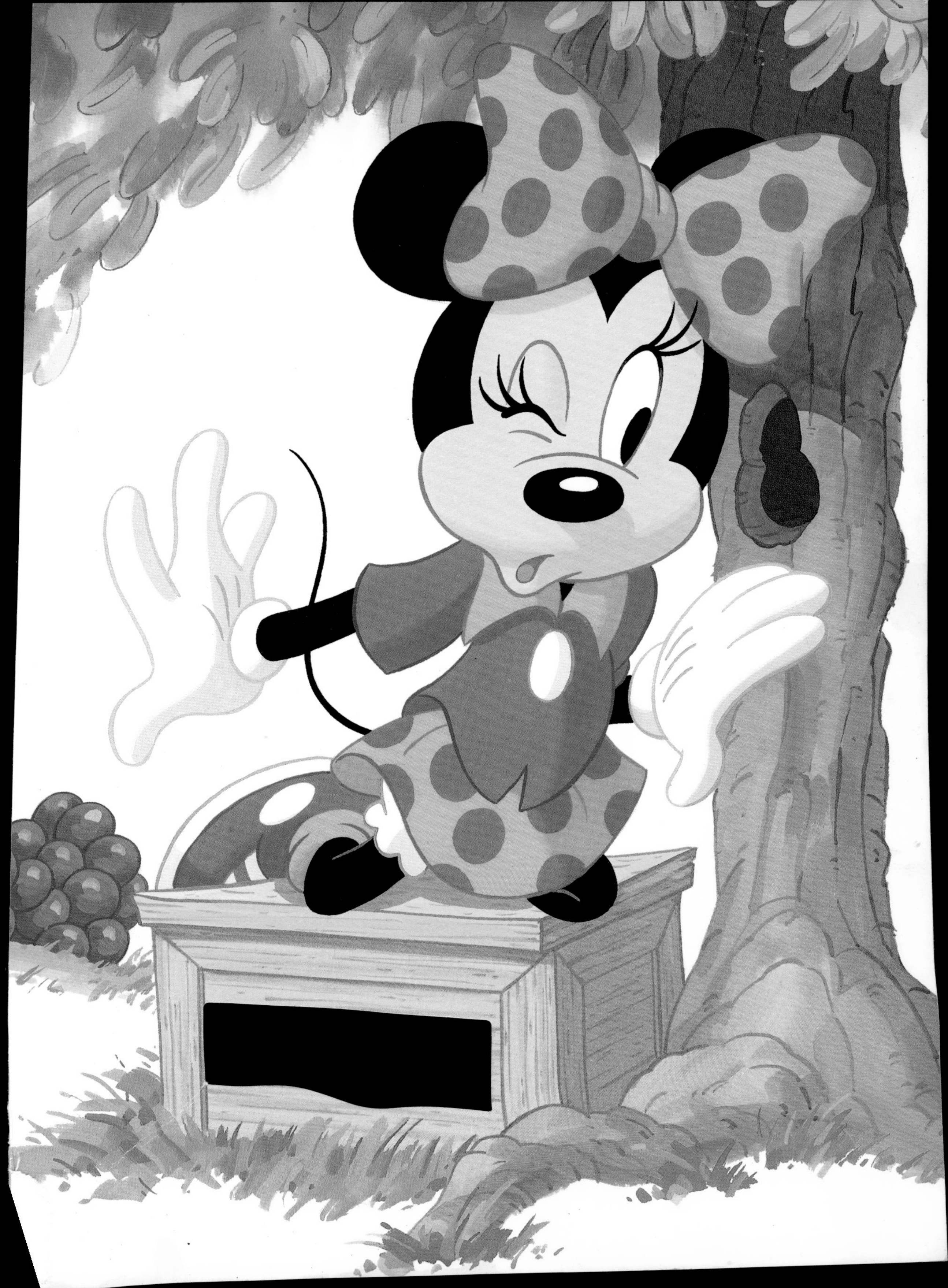

"Well, there sure isn't any basket in this leaky old boat," grumbles Donald. "All I can find is water, water, and more water."

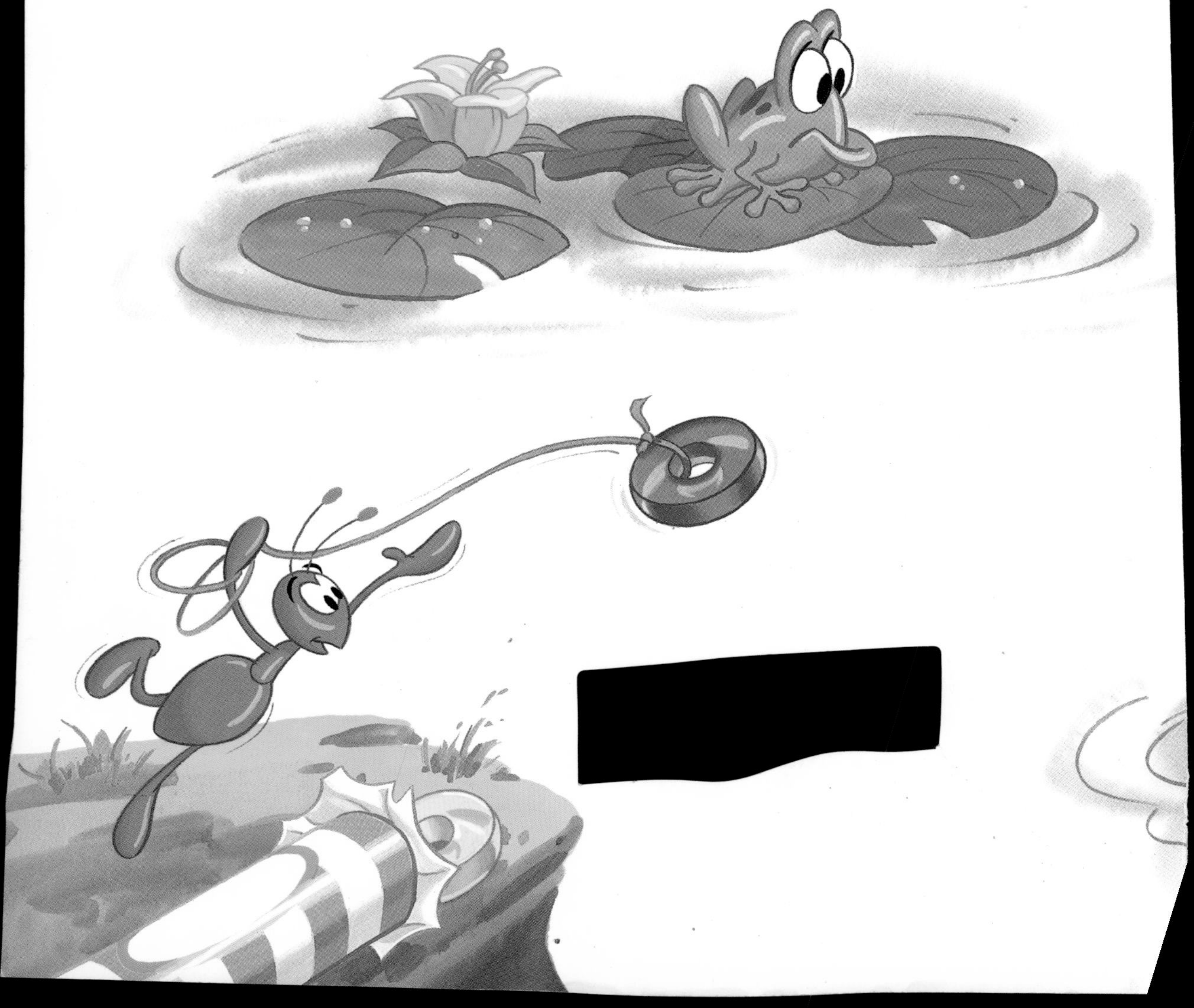

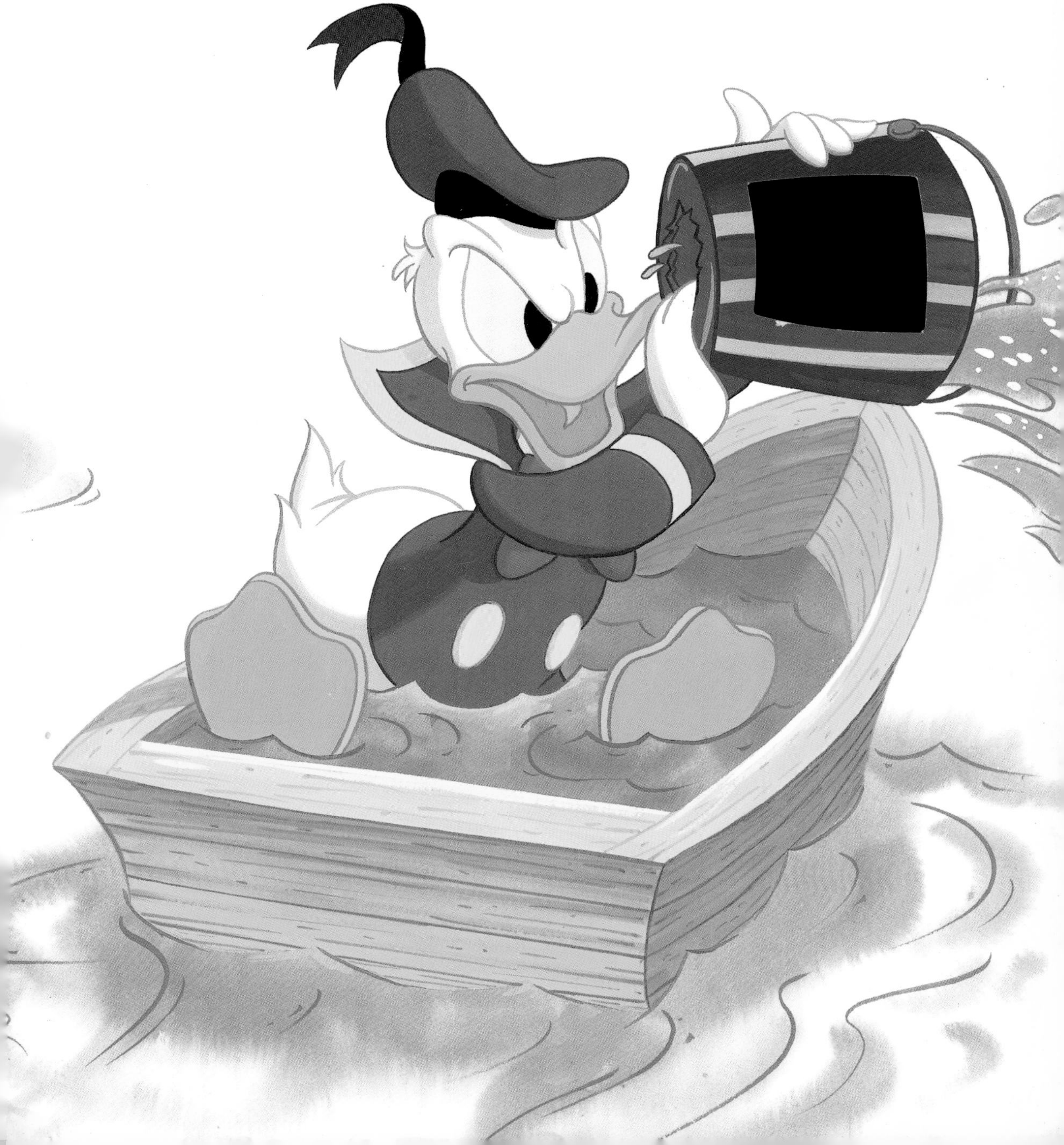

"Hey, gang!" says Mickey. "Is this hole big enough to hide a picnic basket full of food?"

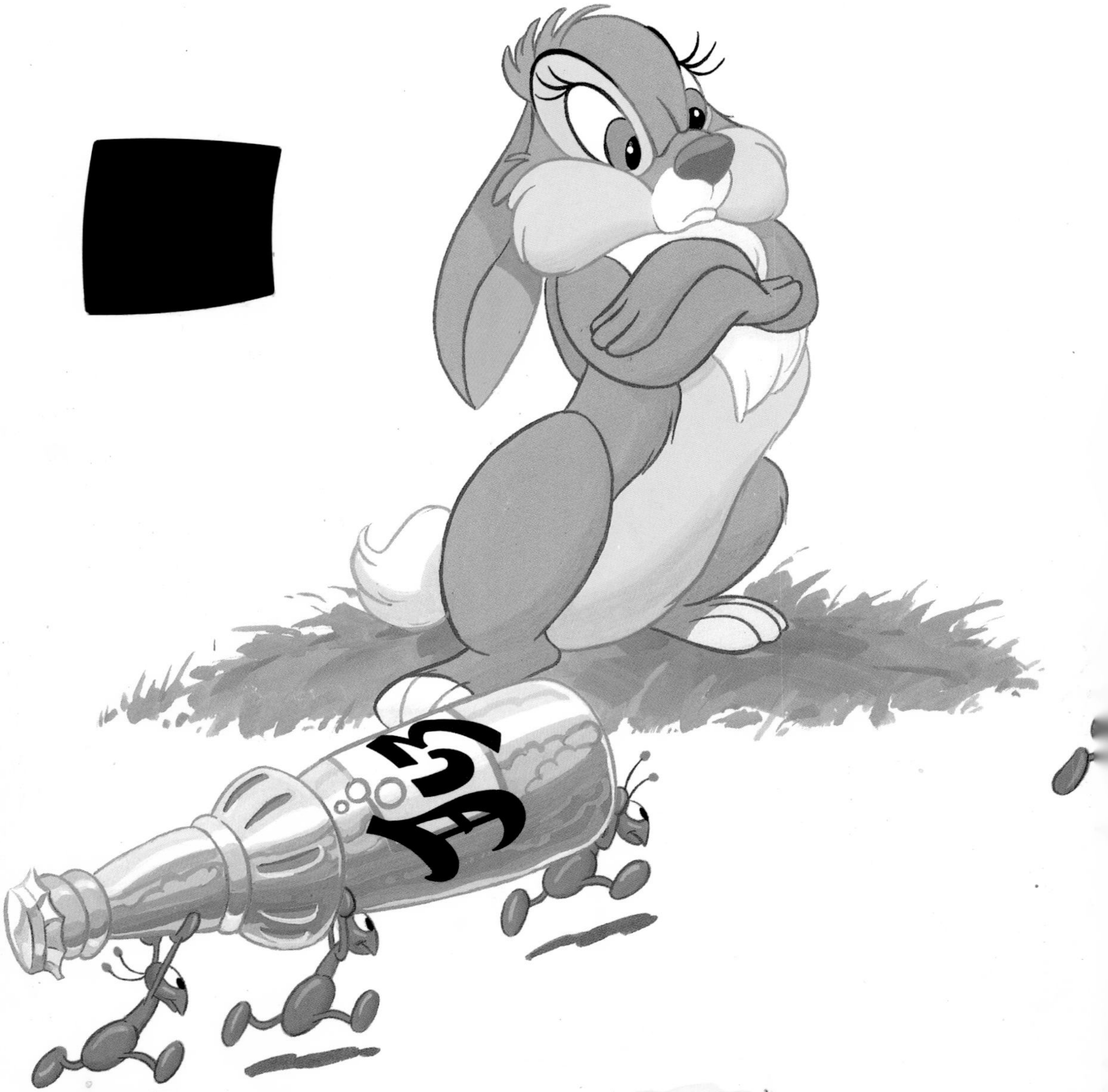

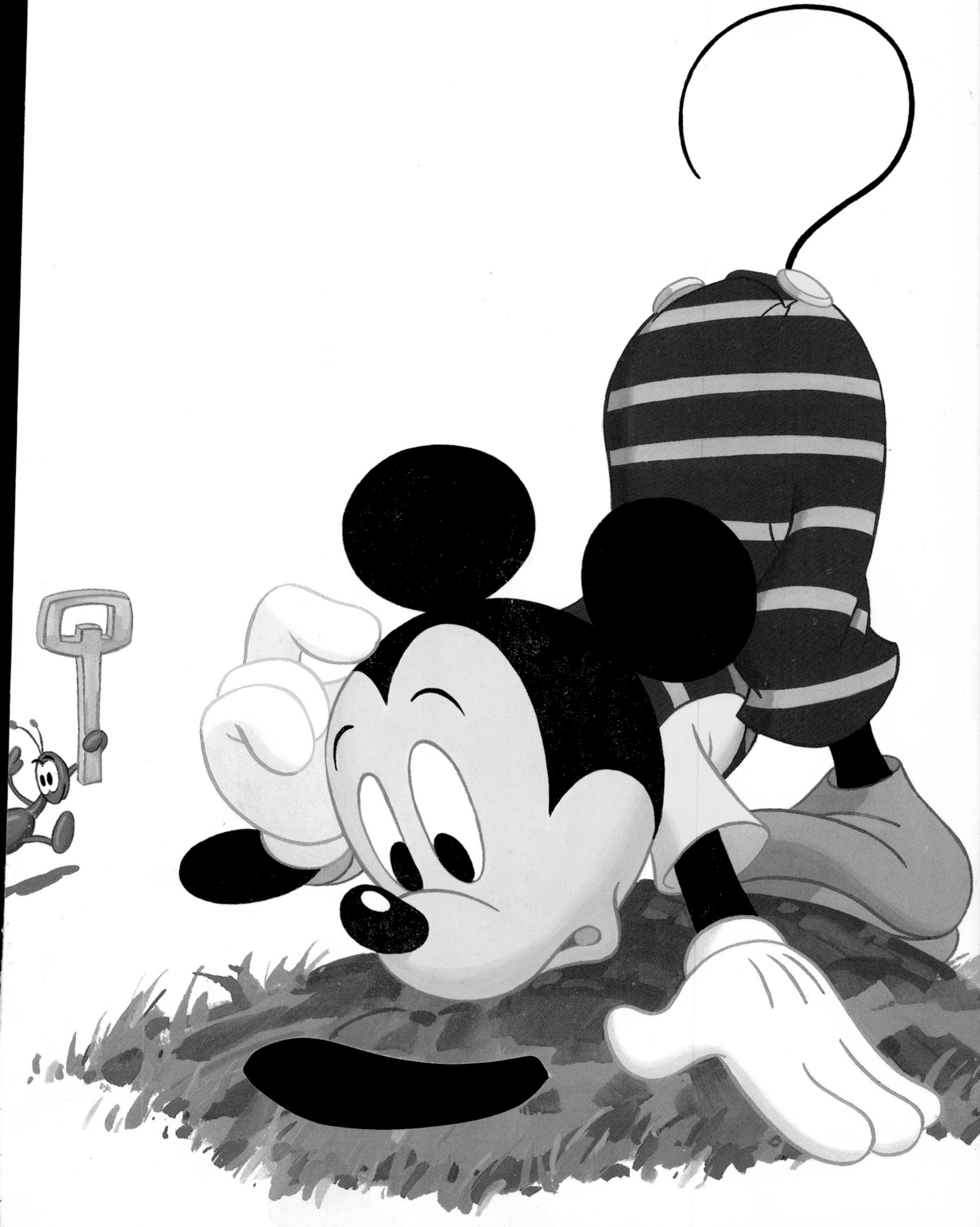

“What hole? What picnic basket? What food?” asks Goofy. “Gawrsh!”

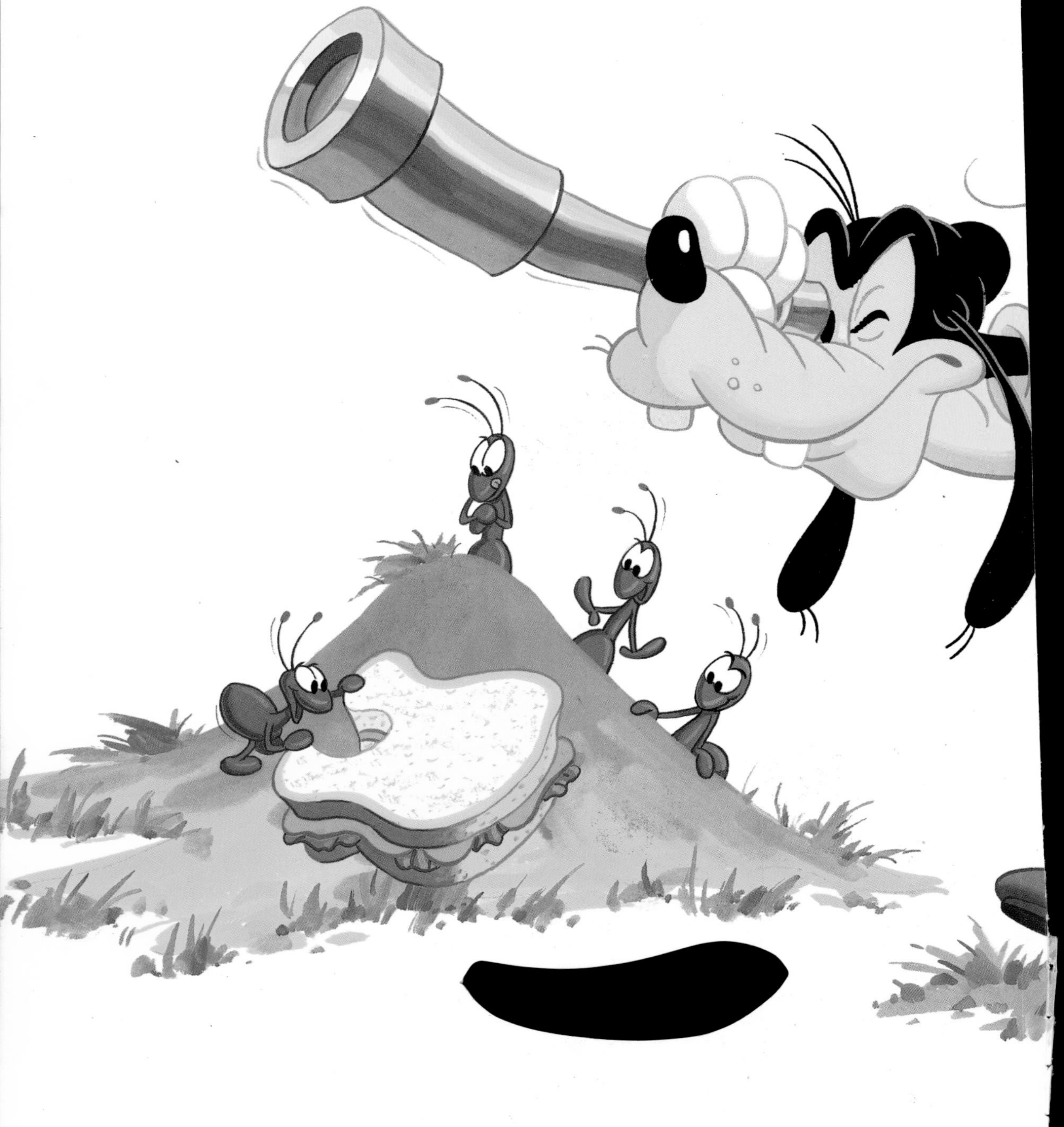

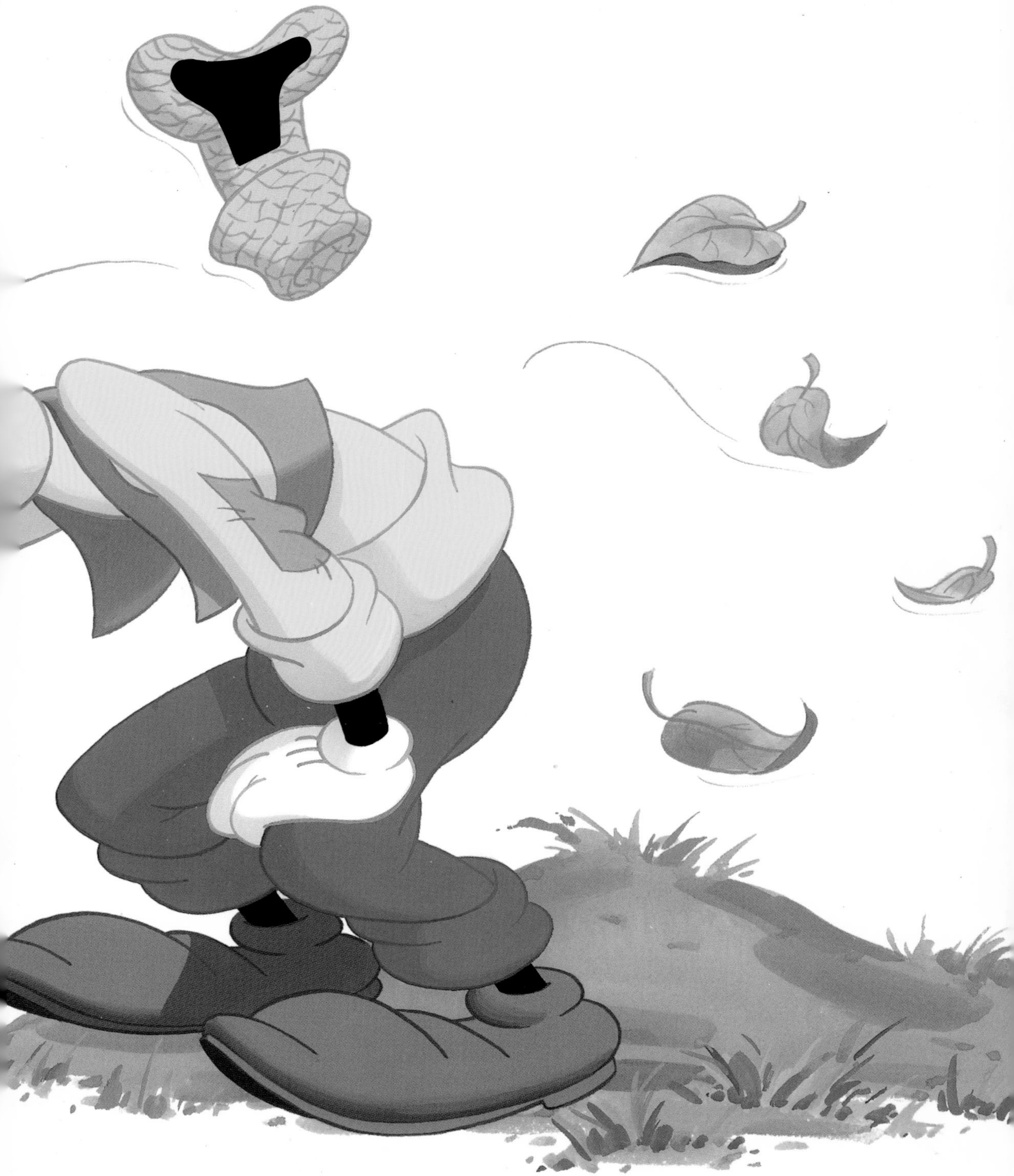

"C'mon everybody!" says Daisy.
"Somebody's eating! My tummy's
growling like a bear! Let's go! "

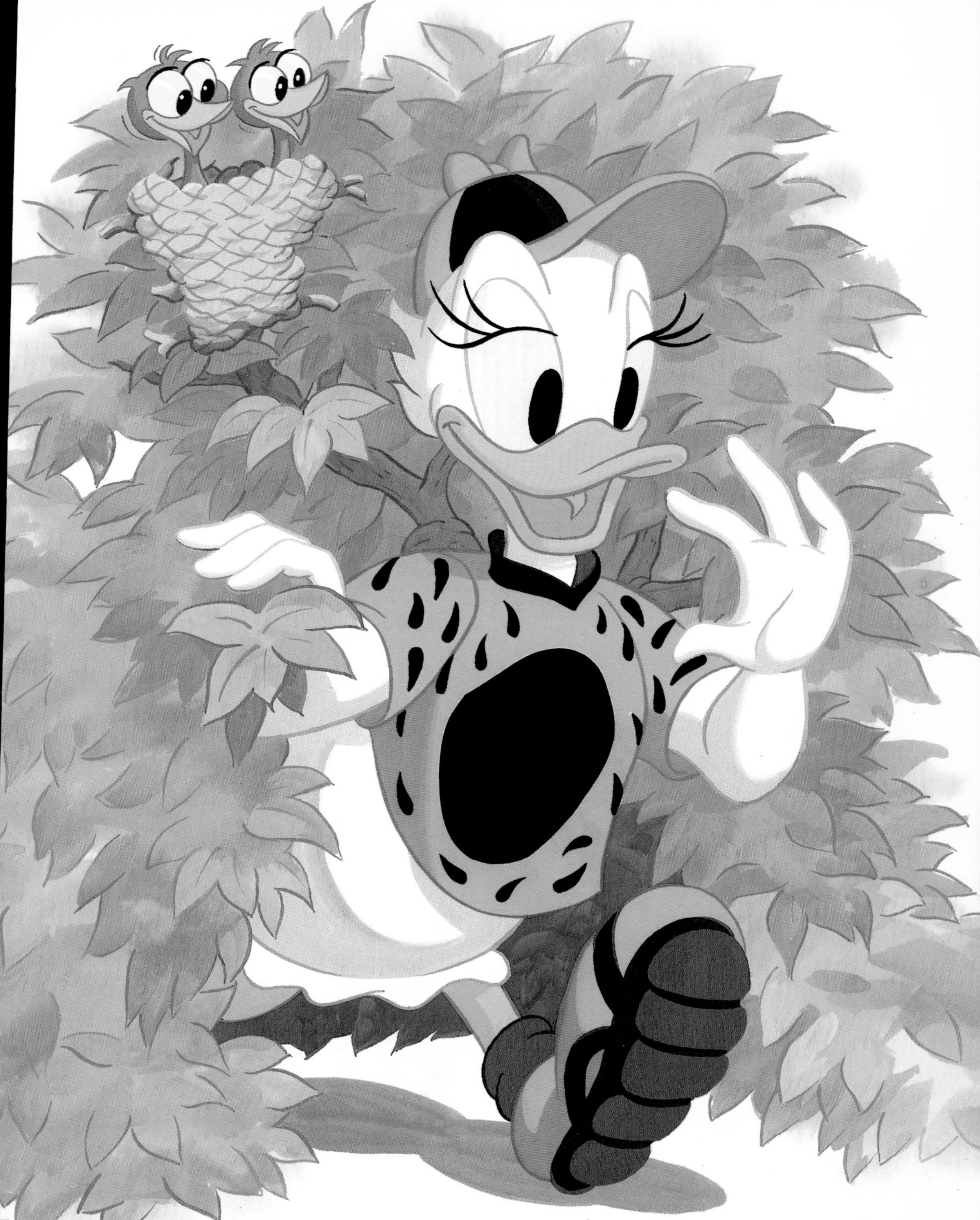

"Well, look what I found," chuckles Mickey. "And there is even some food left for us! Let's eat!"

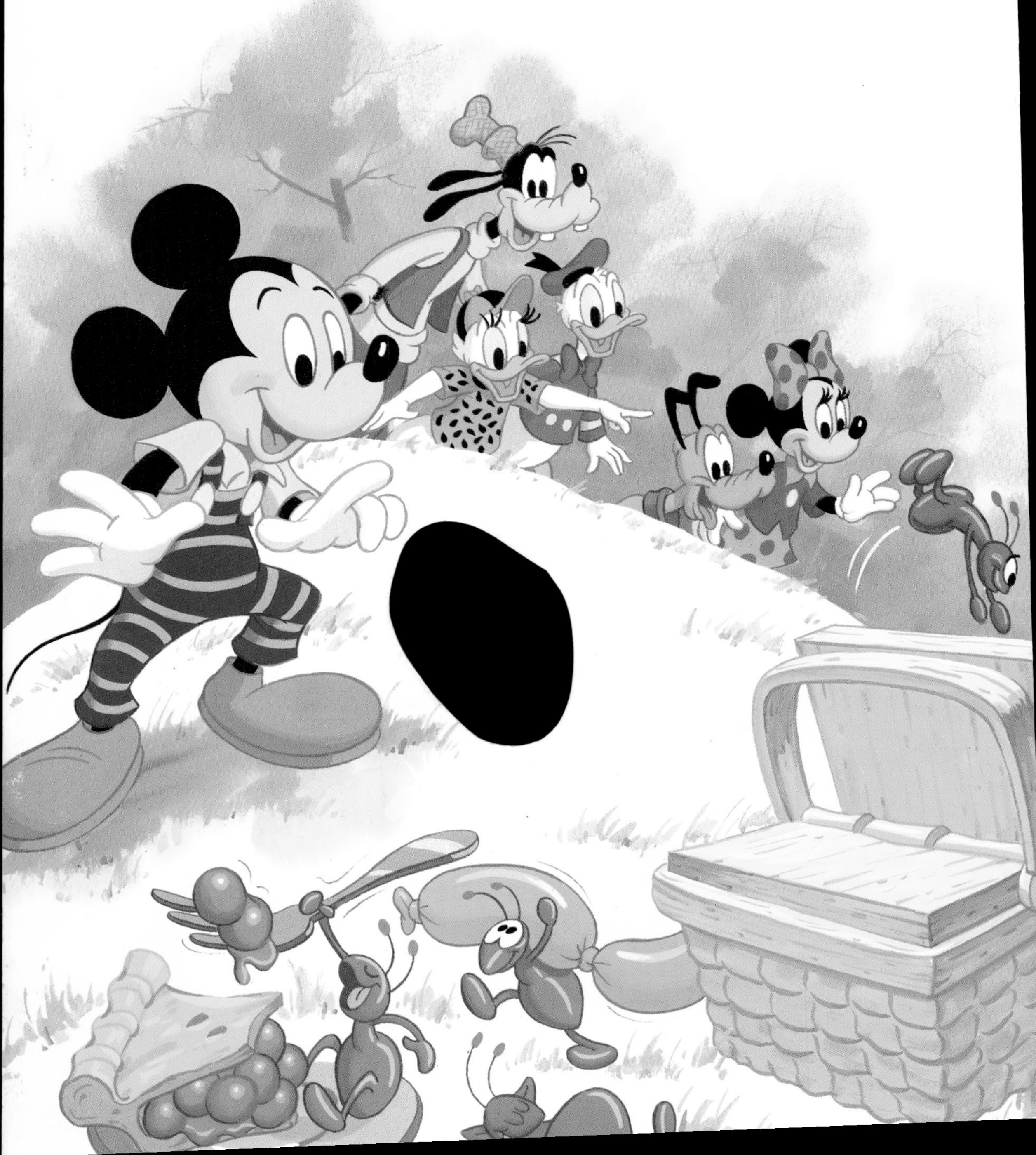

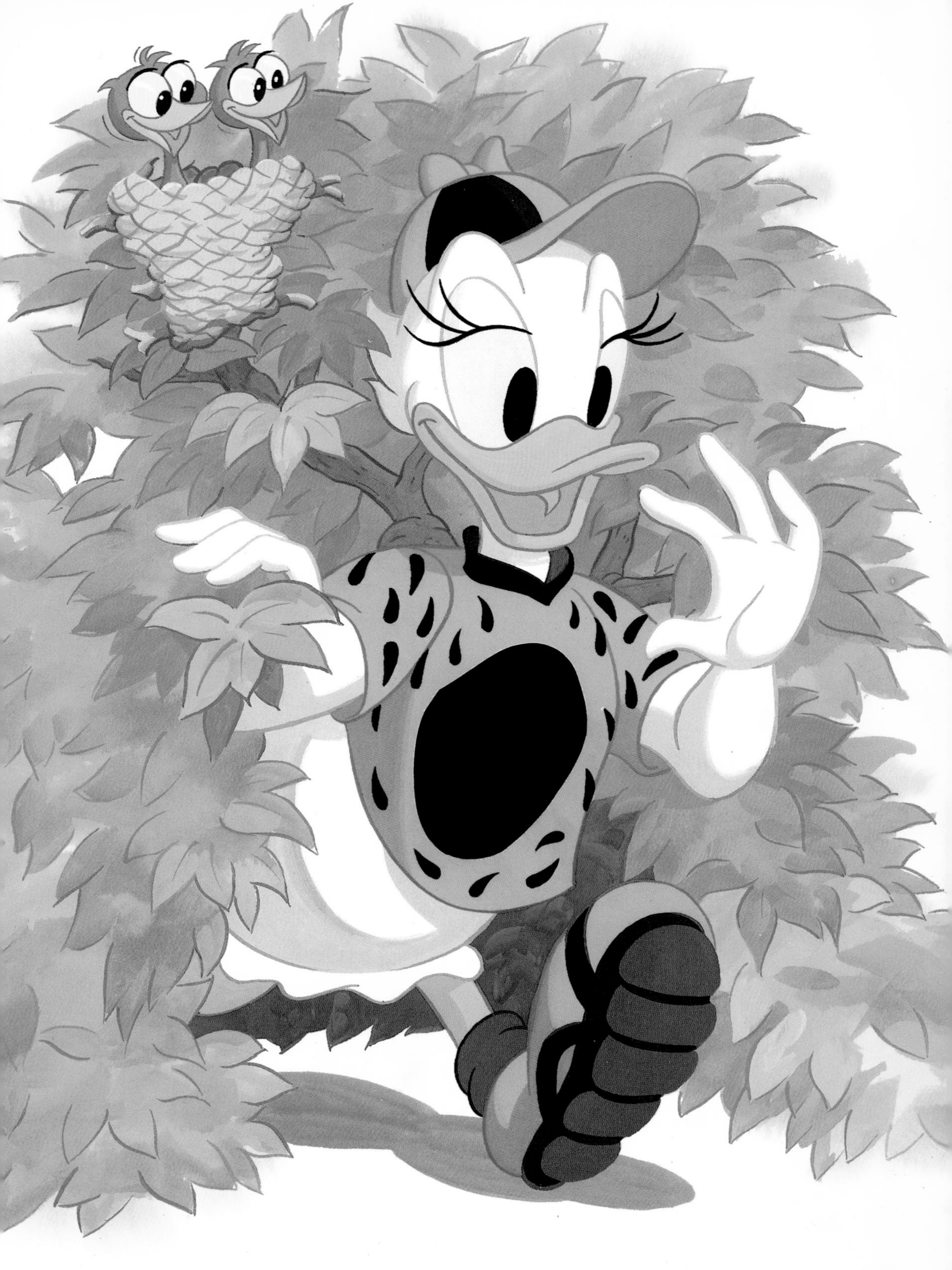

"Well, look what I found," chuckles Mickey.
"And there is even some food left for us! Let's eat!"

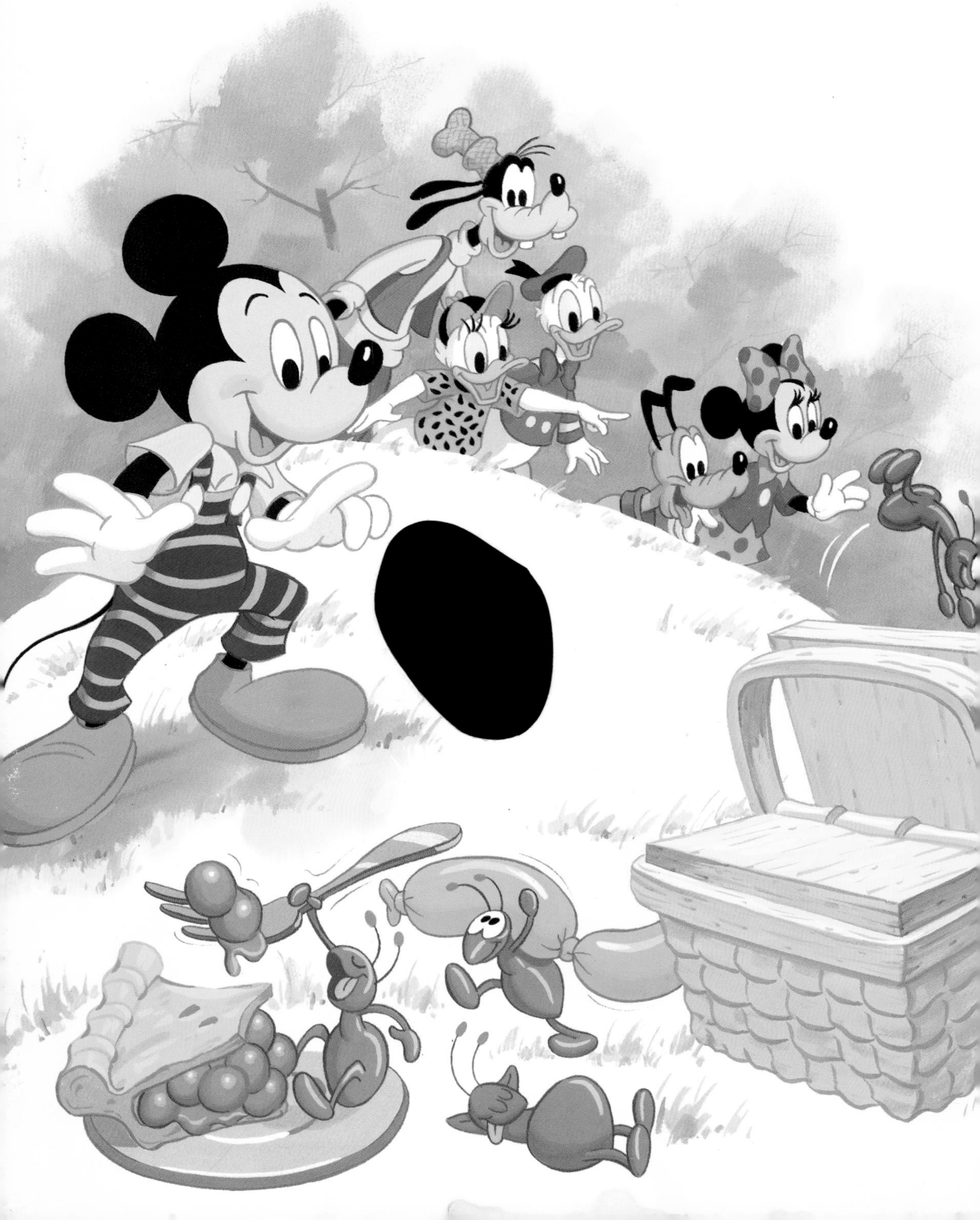